Word List

Here is a list of words that might make it easier to read this book. You'll find them in boldface the first time they appear in the story.

divorce	duh-VORS
conversation	kon-ver-SAY-shun
scrambled	SCRAM-buhld
counselor	KOUN-suh-ler
ceiling	SEE-ling
macaroni	ma-kuh-ROH-nee
activity	ak-TI-vuh-tee
syrup	SER-uhp
materials	muh-TEAR-ee-uls
challenged	CHA-luhnjd
pierced	pearst
umbrellas	uhm-BRE-luhs
fidgety	FI-juh-tee
ruined	ROO-uhned
reassured	re-uh-SHERD
hesitantly	HE-zuh-tent-lee

Barbie™

A Place Called Home

BARBIE and associated trademarks are owned by and used under license from Mattel, Inc. © 1999 Mattel, Inc. All Rights Reserved.
Published by Grolier Books, a division of Grolier Enterprises, Inc.
Story by Linda Williams Aber, Julie Temple Stan, and Agnes Priscsak.
Photo crew: Scott Fujikawa, Mary Hirahara, Glen Bradley, Damon Dulas, and Judy Tsuno.
Produced by Bumpy Slide Books.
Printed in the United States of America.
ISBN: 0-7172-8861-7

GROLIER
B O O K S

Chapter One

"Choose any seat you'd like, young lady!" the bus driver said. He pointed to the empty rows of seats in back of him. "I'm Mr. Reilly. You must be Lisa, right? You're the first name on my list."

"Yes," Lisa replied, a bit nervously. She grabbed her backpack and climbed up into the small, blue bus. As she stepped in, Lisa caught her bag on the door. It pulled her backward.

"Gotcha!" her dad said, catching her.

"Thanks, Dad," Lisa said, pushing her brown hair out of her eyes. "I'm okay."

"Then smile!" her dad said. "Camp

Sunnydale will be great. It's only for two weeks."

"Two weeks!" Lisa moaned. "That's forever!"

The bus driver laughed. "First time away?"

Lisa wasn't sure how to answer the question. This wasn't her first time away. But it was her first time away since her parents' **divorce.**

"The time will fly by," her father said. "When camp is over, your mom will meet the bus and bring you back to her house. Be good, and have fun."

Lisa hugged her dad one last time. Then she climbed onto the bus. She chose a seat and put her bag next to her. That way she wouldn't have to sit next to anyone.

The bus pulled away. Lisa pressed her face against the window. Her father was waving good-bye. She watched him until he was out of sight.

Minutes later, the bus stopped. Four boys piled in, talking and laughing. They marched past Lisa to the very back of the bus. "Good-bye, home. Hello, Camp Sunnydale!" one cheered.

"We're free!" another boy shouted after the bus had pulled away. "No more lawn mowing! No more—"

A curve in the road cut their **conversation** short. "Whoa!" they cried as they leaned first to the left, then to the right.

Lisa scrunched down in her seat. She pulled her collar up over her ears. It wasn't the noise of the boys she was trying to block out. It was her own thoughts that were bothering her. Her parents' divorce this year was bad enough. Then they decided to send her away. Now every bump in the road carried her farther from her parents and closer to a place she'd never been before.

When the bus stopped again, Lisa peeked out over the tops of the seats. She was curious to see who was getting on. Three girls just about Lisa's age were stepping onto the bus.

"Hi, Mr. Reilly," said a pretty girl with black hair and brown eyes.

"We told you we'd see you this summer!" the second girl added. She had short, red hair.

"And here we are!" said the last girl. Her eyes sparkled in her freckled face. She brushed her brown bangs out of her eyes.

The bus driver laughed as the three girls crammed into two seats right behind him. "Janet, Amanda, and Katie, right?" the driver asked.

"Right," they answered.

"I'd like you to meet Lisa," the driver said. "She's new with us this year. And you already know the boys, I think."

Amanda and Janet called "Hi!" over their shoulders. But the brown-haired girl turned around in her seat. "First time at camp?" Katie asked Lisa. Right away she added, "You'll love it!" Then Katie called to one of the noisy boys in the back, "Hi, Brad!"

"Oh, hi, Katie!" the boy in the window seat replied. "Ready to race me again in the lake?"

"Sure!" Katie laughed. "If you don't mind losing two years in a row!"

That sent the boys into a wave of laughter, but Katie turned her attention back to Lisa. "Want to sit with us?" she asked.

"That's okay," Lisa replied. "I like this seat."

"Okay," Katie said, shrugging her shoulders.

Lisa took a sketchbook out of her bag. Katie tried again to get her to join them. But Lisa pretended to be too interested in what she was doing.

"I guess she doesn't want to be friends with us," Lisa heard Amanda whisper.

"Oh, well," Janet replied. "We tried."

Lisa wanted to shout, "I *do* want to be friends with you!" But for some reason the words just wouldn't come out. Instead she kept her eyes on the book in her lap.

Chapter Two

The bus to Camp Sunnydale slowly filled up. Everyone talked about the summer before. "Camp is our home away from home!" Amanda declared.

Hearing the words *home away from home* bothered Lisa. She already had two homes: one with her mother, one with her father. She didn't need a third one at camp. And none of those homes could be the same as the one she'd had with both of her parents. That home was gone forever.

The three-hour bus ride seemed more like ten hours to Lisa. Finally Brad called out, "There's the sign for Camp Sunnydale!"

Katie, Amanda, and Janet **scrambled** across the bus seats and pressed their faces against the windows. The bus turned onto a dirt road marked by a colorful wooden sign:

CAMP SUNNYDALE
For Boys and Girls

"I'll drop you off first," the driver told the girls. "Barbie said to deliver you right to her. Then I'll take the boys to the other side."

"Barbie!?" Janet cried. "We haven't seen her since the beginning of the summer!"

"Yeah," Katie said. "I can't wait to see her!"

Lisa's curiosity got the better of her. She peeked around her seat and asked, "Who's Barbie?"

Lisa had been so quiet that all three girls were surprised to hear her speak. Janet and Amanda just looked at each other. But Katie jumped at the chance to talk to her.

Katie turned around in her seat. "Barbie's

like a big sister to us!" she told Lisa.

Janet turned around, too, and added, "But she's really the big sister of our friend Stacie."

"Oh, don't mention Stacie!" Katie moaned. "You'll make us miss her too much."

Amanda sighed. "Yes, but Stacie is lucky to be going on vacation with Whitney's family. Besides, we'll have fun with Barbie anyway."

Katie continued, "Barbie's the assistant director of the camp. Plus she's the art **counselor.**"

"There she is!" Janet cried. "Hey, Barbie!" she said, knocking on the window. "Barbie!"

Lisa peered across the aisle and out the window. Katie pointed toward a tall, blond woman who was smiling and waving. She wore a whistle around her neck and held a clipboard in her hand. "That's Barbie," Katie explained.

The bus stopped at the girls' sign-in area. "Hello!" Barbie shouted as the girls poured out of the bus. "Welcome to Camp Sunnydale!"

Katie, Amanda, and Janet raced over to meet her.

"How was the ride?" Barbie asked.

"Great!" Katie replied. She gave Barbie a hug. "We met a new girl named Lisa."

Lisa was a few steps behind the others. She took a deep breath and walked over to Barbie.

"You must be Lisa," Barbie said to her. "I'm glad you're here."

"So am I," Lisa answered slowly. "If only," she thought, "that were true."

Barbie went to greet the rest of the campers. Lisa looked around. Girls were everywhere. And everyone seemed to know each other. A million questions raced through Lisa's head. "Where am I going to sleep? What am I supposed to do with my bag? When will I start to fit in? How am I ever going to feel comfortable so far from home?"

"You look a little lost," Barbie said, walking back over to Lisa. "Don't worry. You'll soon get to know where everything is." Barbie checked her

clipboard. "You'll be in the same cabin as Katie, Amanda, and Janet. Your cabin counselor, Nikki, will take you there."

Katie overheard what Barbie had said. "I don't remember Nikki from last year."

"She's new," Barbie explained. Then she called over her shoulder, "Nikki! Come meet your cabinmates!"

A black-haired young woman in a Camp Sunnydale T-shirt walked over. Barbie introduced Nikki to each of the girls. Secretly, Lisa was glad that she wasn't the only new face in the group. "We'll be in the Chatty Chipmunks cabin," Nikki told her campers. "Ready to go?"

"Definitely!" Katie bubbled. She picked up her duffel bag and groaned. "Ooof!" she said as she slung it over her shoulder.

Janet laughed. "I thought you said you were going to pack lighter this year."

Katie grinned and replied, "I did. My stuff

just got heavier."

"Next stop: Chatty Chipmunks!" Nikki announced. "See you later, Barbie!"

The four girls said good-bye to Barbie. Then they followed Nikki down the path through the woods. Katie, Amanda, and Janet chattered all the way to the end of a long row of cabins. The small, brown buildings had screen windows on all sides. The canvas storm flaps had been rolled up. Screen doors slammed as giggling girls skipped in and out of the cabins.

Suddenly Janet shouted, "Here it is!"

The girls carried their bags inside the cabin.

"Ah, camp life!" Amanda sighed.

Lisa looked around the room. There were five beds and five dressers. Nikki's area was set apart from the others. A shoebox marked *Letters from Home* was open on her bed, and a half-written letter was next to it.

"Pick your parking place," Nikki told the girls, pointing to the other beds. On each bed was a pillow and a neatly folded blanket.

Lisa waited to see which beds the other girls would choose. Janet and Amanda chose two beds next to each other. Katie put her bag down on the bed closest to the wall.

"I guess you'll be with me," Katie said to Lisa. "Don't worry. I promise I won't snore!"

With that, Amanda, Janet, and Katie got into a snoring contest. Lisa couldn't help joining in. Snorting like pigs, they fell onto their beds, laughing.

"Okay, girls," Nikki began in her most official camp counselor voice. "It's time to go over the camp rules." The girls were still giggling as Nikki picked up her clipboard and began reading. "'Never go anywhere without telling somebody. Always leave a place cleaner than you found it. Lights out by nine o'clock.'" When Nikki finished going over the rules, she said, "Now let's get organized!"

"You mean SNORE-ganized!" Katie joked, bringing on another round of giggles.

"Organized, snore-ganized," Nikki laughed. "Either way, you'll want to be unpacked before the supper bell rings."

Lisa's laughter stopped. She lay faceup on her bed and stared at the **ceiling.** "Supper," she thought. "What kind of food will they have at camp?" If she were home at her mother's house, they'd probably have chicken. Or if she were home at her father's house, they'd probably have spaghetti. Thinking of her two homes suddenly gave Lisa a double dose of homesickness.

While she was lying there thinking, the other girls were busy unpacking. Lisa had to rush to catch up.

"I'm finished," Katie told Lisa. "Do you want some help?"

"Okay," Lisa replied. She handed Katie a stack of T-shirts. They worked quickly to put everything away.

"That's it, I guess," Lisa declared.

"What's this?" Katie asked. She pointed at a big pad of heavy paper sticking out of Lisa's bag.

"My sketchbook," Lisa answered. "You can look at it if you want to."

Katie sat down on Lisa's bed and opened the book. "Wow!" she exclaimed. She was looking at a pastel drawing of a house and a garden full of colorful flowers. "This is so pretty!"

"What is?" Amanda asked, walking over.

Katie held the book so Amanda could see. She slowly turned the pages. Janet and Nikki gathered around, too. Page after page showed sketches of houses in all styles. "You're really good at drawing!" Janet pointed out.

"You've got talent!" Nikki declared.

Lisa glowed. She was glad that they liked her drawings. Just then the supper bell rang.

"Anyone hungry?" Nikki asked.

"Starving!" Janet answered for the group.

All the other campers were hungry, too. Twenty tables in the Food Barn were filled with boys and girls. The smell of **macaroni** and cheese filled the air. The girls from Chatty Chipmunks were eating when Barbie came over to their table. "Hi!" she said. "May I join you?"

"Sure!" the girls agreed.

Barbie pulled up a seat next to Lisa. "So is everyone settled in?" she asked.

All the girls replied at once. But Lisa was silent. Her attention was on the Little Ladybugs table. A little girl at the table was crying. Her counselor was trying to cheer her up.

"Poor Lucy," Barbie sighed. "She's been crying since she got here this morning. We had to call her mother to come and take her home."

Katie gasped. "On her first day?"

"Some kids just aren't ready for sleep-away camp," Barbie replied. "Don't forget that Lucy's younger than you girls."

"Oh," said Janet, nodding, "that's why."

Dessert brought Lisa's attention back to her own table. As they went to get brownies and ice cream, Barbie said good night. "Sleep well, girls. I'll see you tomorrow at the Art Barn. I think art is your first **activity** of the day."

The girls said good night to Barbie. After dessert, they walked back toward their cabin. As they passed the first cabin, the door opened. Lisa looked back to see who was coming out. It was little Lucy. She wore pajamas and held a teddy bear in one hand. Her other hand held her mother's.

"It's all right, Lucy," the girl's mother said, stroking her shiny hair. "You'll be home in your own bed before you know it!"

"Lucky duck!" Lisa thought. She hurried back to her cabin, where the other girls were already inside. Everybody was tired. They made the short walk together to the Bath Barn to brush their teeth. Then Nikki and the girls crawled into their beds. Everyone chatted for a little while before drifting off to sleep.

But Lisa couldn't sleep. It was too quiet without the talking and laughing of the other girls. In the darkness, she felt very alone. She climbed out of bed and tiptoed to the window. Moonlight sparkled on the lake. In the distance, she could see tiny car headlights. Lisa couldn't help but wish that one of those cars would come for her. A tear rolled down her cheek. Then again, no car could bring her back to the home she missed the most—the home she'd had when her parents were still together.

Chapter Three

Sunlight streamed in through the window screens. Lisa opened her eyes and realized the long, lonely night was over. She closed her eyes again and pulled her scratchy wool blanket over her head.

Nikki was already dressed in her red bathing suit and shorts. "Time to get up, sleepyheads," she told her campers. "Art is your first activity today. And Barbie will be waiting."

"Morning, Nikki," Katie and Amanda said together.

Janet threw back her covers and jumped out

of bed. "Brrrrr!" she shivered. "It's freezing!"

Nikki laughed. "There's nothing like cold morning air to wake you up *really* fast." She went over to Lisa's bed and shook her gently. "Are you awake, Lisa?"

"I guess so," Lisa groaned.

"You will be once your feet touch the floor," Katie cried. She hopped around on the cold wood floor, her teeth chattering.

Yawns, giggles, and sounds from shivering girls echoed up and down the row of cabins. Camp Sunnydale was awake. And now, so was Lisa. When they were all dressed and ready, Nikki and the girls headed for the Food Barn.

"We'd better hurry," Katie said. "If we don't get there first, the boys will use up all the **syrup.**"

When they stepped inside the Food Barn, a girl waved to them. "Katie, Janet, Amanda! Over here!" she shouted. She was pointing to some empty seats next to her.

Katie waved back and told Lisa, "That's Tricia. We know her from last year. Want to go sit with her?"

Even though Lisa wanted to join Katie, she answered, "I'm not really that hungry. I'll just grab a muffin." Then she added, "Would you tell Nikki that I'll meet up with you at the Art Barn?"

"Okay," Katie said, shrugging her shoulders. "See you later."

At the Art Barn, Barbie was outside rinsing a bucket with water. She looked up to see Lisa slowly walking up the path. "Hi, there!" she called. "Another early riser, huh? Want to help me get things ready?"

Lisa smiled shyly and stuffed the last bite of muffin in her mouth. "Okay," she mumbled.

Barbie and Lisa set out paints, chalk, clay, and **materials** for puppets. The two chatted about art as they worked. Just as they were finishing, Lisa's cabinmates arrived. Katie, Amanda, and Janet hurried inside to choose seats at the same worktable.

"You sit here, Lisa," said Katie, patting the seat next to her. Lisa grinned at Katie and sat down. Each camper began working on her own special project. The boys from the Tardy Turtles cabin arrived late. Katie was making a bowl out of clay. Janet and Amanda were cutting scraps of cloth to make puppets. Lisa was busy sketching the moonlit lake. She tried to remember how it had looked the night before.

Barbie walked around helping all of the boys and girls. When she got to Lisa, she patted her on the shoulder and said, "Thanks for helping me this morning." Then she looked at Lisa's drawing and added, "You have a lot of talent."

"Really?" Lisa asked. She wanted to hear more, but the cleanup bell rang.

"Where do we go next?" Katie asked Nikki.

The counselor looked at her clipboard and replied, "Amanda and Janet, you have horseback riding. Katie and Lisa, you have swimming."

"All right!" exclaimed Katie, clapping her hands together. "It's time for my race against Brad in the lake. When I'm done with him, he'll be doing the dead man's float. Come on, Lisa!"

The girls giggled and started to leave. But Nikki held up her hand. "Wait! Let's all plan to meet at noon for lunch."

Everyone agreed. Amanda and Janet left for the Riding Barn. The others grabbed their towels and headed for the lake.

"Follow me," Katie called as the cabin door slammed behind her. She started running down the path to the lake. Lisa and Nikki hurried to catch up.

Just then they heard a sound. *Cheep! Cheep!*

The girls stopped running and looked around.

Soon Lisa found where the noise was coming from. "It's a baby bird!" she cried. "It must have fallen out of its nest." Lisa knelt down. But as she gently reached for the bird, a loud squawking sound from above stopped her.

"Wait!" Nikki warned. "The mother is trying to scare us away from it."

"Yikes!" said Katie, backing up. "She looks mad!"

"The bird is young, but it's not really a baby. It already has feathers, see?" Nikki pointed out.

They quietly watched the birds for a while. Then Nikki said, "I don't think the little bird fell out of its nest. I think the mother pushed it out."

Lisa gasped. "That's terrible! The bird is still so tiny!"

"Yes, but sometimes that's the only way the mother can teach her baby to fly," Nikki explained. "A bird can't learn to fly sitting in its nest, you know."

"I never thought of it that way," Lisa admitted. Nikki and the girls watched the bird flutter its wings and lift up off the ground a bit.

"Okay," Katie cried, changing the subject. "Last one in the lake is a rotten egg!"

With her head start, Katie beat Lisa and Nikki to the water. She stripped to the bathing suit she wore under her clothes and plunged into the water. She swam up to Brad and **challenged** him to a race. Soon they both were swimming out to a raft in the middle of the lake.

Lisa stopped short at the water's edge. She took off her shoes and socks and felt the water with one toe. "Brrr!" she thought. "How did Katie dive in like that?" Slowly she finished undressing and took a deep breath.

Suddenly a loud, sharp whistle **pierced** the air. The lifeguards were waving for everyone to come in to shore. Dark clouds were rolling in from across the lake.

"Everyone out of the water!" a lifeguard shouted. "A storm is coming!"

Lisa picked up her clothes. "Too bad," she thought. "This was just beginning to look like fun."

Fat raindrops began to fall. Holding their towels over their heads like **umbrellas,** Katie, Lisa, and Nikki hurried back up the path. When they reached the spot where they'd seen the bird on the ground, Lisa stopped.

"Come on," Katie called, pulling Lisa by the arm.

"Just a minute," Lisa answered. She looked on the ground, but the little bird was gone. She couldn't find it anywhere. "Oh, no!" Lisa thought. "What's going to happen if the little bird can't find its home? It could be all alone in the storm!"

"Lisa!" Nikki called from the top of the path. "Hurry!"

Chapter Four

Katie, Lisa, and Nikki tumbled through the cabin doorway just as a giant clap of thunder boomed behind them.

"Aaahh!" the campers screamed. It started to pour. Janet and Amanda were already back from horseback riding. They were playing a game of cards on Janet's bed.

"We made it!" Nikki stated. "It's really coming down out there! We'll have to make the best of it until the sun comes back out."

"You mean *if* it comes back out," Katie added.

Lisa thought about the bird and frowned.

She was worried. The little bird had looked scared. She was sure it had wanted to stay in its nest. That was its home, where it was safe. "Nikki," Lisa said out loud, "I couldn't find the little bird back on the path. What will happen to it in the storm?"

"Maybe it flew back to its nest," Nikki said.

Katie shook her head and replied, "It didn't look like it was ready to fly yet."

"Well," Nikki continued, "then I guess it will be at the mercy of the weather. It will have to find a safe place to wait out the storm." Lisa bit her lip. She didn't like the sound of that.

At first it felt cozy being inside together with the rain coming down outside. Nikki wrote letters while Amanda read a book. Katie and Janet played checkers. Lisa tried to finish one of her sketches, but she didn't get very far. She kept getting up to see if the rain had stopped. It hadn't. It was raining when the campers went to lunch.

It was still raining when the supper bell rang.

Even with umbrellas, everyone's clothes got soaked. After dinner the whole camp gathered to watch a movie. But the roof of the Food Barn was leaking. The counselors placed metal pots out to catch the drips. Soon the *ping, ping, ping* of the dripping water was drowning out the movie. Lisa felt like it was even raining inside.

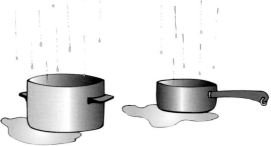

Afterward, Barbie announced their rainy-day schedules for the next day. Then everyone ran back to their cabins for the evening.

That night campers at Camp Sunnydale fell asleep to the sound of wind and rain. They woke up to more of the same. For the next two days, all outdoor activities were rained out.

By the third day, the coziness of being

inside had worn off. Everyone had come down with a bad case of cabin fever. That night the *ping, ping, ping* of the rain wasn't the only thing drowning out the movie. The campers were noisy and **fidgety.** The girls from Chatty Chipmunks decided to leave the movie early.

As they sloshed back toward their cabin, the girls began to complain.

"I miss my dog, Sundance," Janet sighed. "I wish I were home!"

"Me, too," Amanda sniffed. "I could be making cookies with my nana!"

"I'm even beginning to miss my little brother," Katie admitted. "This camp should be called Camp Rainydale."

"I bet that little bird misses its home, too," Lisa added softly.

Since the rain had started, Nikki had noticed a change in Lisa. She had been spending more time with her sketchbook and less time with the other girls. Lisa's sketchbook was now almost overflowing with drawings, mostly of houses.

Nikki thought for a moment. Then she told her campers, "I need to see Barbie about something. You have a bit of free time before you have to get ready for bed. It might make you all feel better to write some letters home. I'll have the counselor from Little Ladybugs look in on you. Lights out by nine o'clock. Promise?"

"We promise," the girls repeated as they ran down the path.

Once they were inside their cabin, the girls dried off. Amanda plopped down on her bed. Instantly she jumped back up. "How did my bed get wet?" she cried.

"Oh, no," Janet moaned. "Now the cabin roof must be leaking, too."

The other girls ran to check their things.

Lisa hurried over to her area. She noticed that her sketchbook had been left on her bed. She went to pick it up and realized that it was sopping wet. "Oh, my drawings!" Lisa cried.

Janet saw Lisa flipping through her **ruined** book. The once-beautiful drawings were now blurry. The rain had made the colors blend together. The outlines of the many houses she had drawn had almost disappeared. Janet looked at her feet. "I just wanted to show Tricia your great drawings," she confessed. "I forgot to put your book back. I'm really sorry."

Everyone looked up from what they were doing. A silence filled the room.

"I hate this place!" Lisa whispered angrily.

Katie sighed. "Well," she said, "at least it started out as a perfect week."

"But it ended up being perfectly *terrible*," Lisa muttered.

No one said another word about the sketchbook. The girls set out a bucket to catch the leaks. Then everyone went to bed.

Chapter Five

Meanwhile, Nikki had finished speaking to the counselor of the Little Ladybugs. Then she splashed through the puddles to Barbie's cabin. She knocked on the screen door.

"Come in," Barbie called, holding a mop. "I hope you don't mind getting your feet wet."

Nikki shook off her umbrella and stepped inside. "Too late. They're already soaked, like everything else."

Barbie continued mopping the floor. "The rain sure has made everything a mess," she said.

"Especially in my cabin," Nikki replied.

"What's wrong?" Barbie asked, looking up.

Nikki sighed. She pulled up a chair and sat down. "The rain is messing up my campers' fun, Barbie. Everybody's getting homesick. We have to find something to take their minds off the bad weather."

"Why don't we get a project going?" Barbie suggested. "Something everyone can work on."

"Hmmm," Nikki said. "What could we do?"

"I've got it!" Barbie exclaimed, setting her mop down. "We'll make a camp mural. Then we can hang it at our farewell campfire! That's a project we can all work on together indoors."

"Great idea!" Nikki agreed.

"We'll get the campers started on it first thing in the morning," Barbie promised.

"Thanks, Barbie," the younger counselor said. "I knew you'd think of something."

"You're welcome," Barbie answered. Then she grinned. "I've got another idea. Why don't you grab the other mop out of the closet?"

"Okay," Nikki laughed. The two friends chatted as they finished cleaning up.

"Thanks for your help!" Barbie called as Nikki left. The young counselor felt much better as she headed back to Chatty Chipmunks. Nikki tiptoed inside and checked on the sleeping girls. She shined her flashlight on Janet, then on Amanda, then on Katie, and then on—Lisa's pillow!

"Lisa?" Nikki whispered loudly. "Are you in here?"

But Lisa's bed was empty. Lisa was gone!

"Katie!" cried Nikki, shaking the girl awake. "Did Lisa say where she was going?"

"Huh?" Katie answered sleepily. "Isn't she in her bed?"

"What's going on?" Janet asked with a yawn.

"Why is everyone up?" Amanda whispered.

"Lisa's missing!" Katie cried.

Nikki thought quickly. "You girls stay here,"

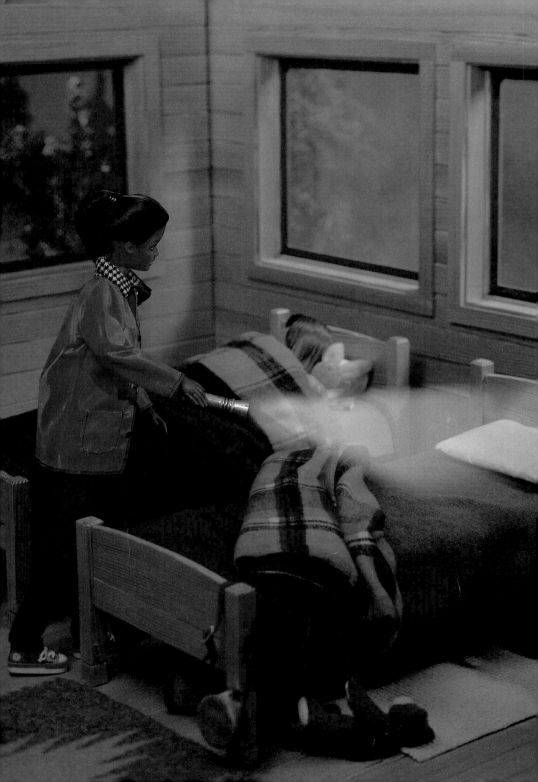

she said. "I'll need to let Barbie and the other staff know that Lisa is gone."

The three girls were very worried. Janet explained to Nikki what had happened to the sketchbook.

"Is Lisa going to be okay?" Katie asked. "It's raining hard out there."

"Don't worry," Nikki **reassured** the girls. "We'll find her."

The Little Ladybugs counselor again promised to check on Nikki's campers. Perhaps Lisa would return to the cabin. The rest of the staff split up, flashlights and umbrellas in hand. Nikki and Barbie went to the Bath Barn. "Lisa?" Nikki called. "Are you in here?"

There was no answer.

Other counselors checked the trails and the campfire clearing. They searched the surrounding woods and the dirt road leading up to the camp. But there was no sign of Lisa.

"I'm worried, Barbie," Nikki confessed. "Where could Lisa be? We've looked everywhere."

"There are still two places left," Barbie said. "Let's split up. You go to the Riding Barn. I'll go to the Food Barn. We'll meet back at your cabin."

"Okay," Nikki agreed. Then she hurried off.

When Barbie arrived at the Food Barn, the building was dark. She went inside. "Lisa?" she called. Her voice echoed through the large, empty room. Barbie listened hard. Suddenly she heard something. *Clink! Clink! Clink!*

Barbie noticed that a light was on down the hall. She walked toward it. As Barbie neared the small office, she saw Lisa. The young girl was shivering in her wet pajamas. She had just finished putting coins into the pay phone. But instead of dialing, she just stood there, holding the receiver to her ear. Finally she hung up.

"Lisa?" Barbie said softly.

Lisa turned around. Barbie could see that

she had been crying. Barbie walked over to the shaking girl and wrapped her jacket around her. Lisa stammered, "Barbie, I . . . I . . ."

"It's okay, Sweetie," Barbie said gently. "You just wanted to call home, right?"

Lisa sniffled and looked down. "Yeah," she replied. "At first I didn't want to come to sleep-away camp. But I met you and Katie, and I thought it would be okay. Then the rain came and ruined all my drawings. That's when I decided to go home. I came here to call my mom. But then I thought about my dad. I miss him, too. You see," she paused and took a deep breath. "My parents don't live together anymore."

"It's okay, I already know," Barbie gently explained.

Lisa looked up at Barbie. Then she blurted out, "When you came in, I was trying to decide who to call first. I miss both of my parents. I don't know what to do."

"Why don't you sleep on it?" Barbie suggested. "If you still want to go home in the morning, we'll call *both* of your parents. Now we need to get you back to your cabin and into some dry clothes."

Shivering, Lisa nodded her head. "Okay," she sighed. Then she hugged Barbie tightly.

As Lisa and Barbie walked back to the cabin, they saw one of the other counselors. Barbie asked him to let everyone know that Lisa was safe. Then she turned to Lisa. "You know, the entire staff is out looking for you."

Lisa's eyes grew wide. "Really?" she asked.

"Really!" Barbie told her. "Everyone has been very worried about you."

"I'm sorry," Lisa said. "I didn't think anyone would care."

Barbie frowned. "Well," she began, "you were wrong. We all care very much. We think of Camp Sunnydale as your home away from home.

We want you to feel safe and happy here."

When they got back to the Chatty Chipmunks cabin, Lisa could see Nikki and her cabinmates huddled on one of the beds. When Lisa walked in, everyone shrieked with delight.

"You're okay!" exclaimed Katie, leaping up to hug Lisa.

"I didn't mean for your sketchbook to get ruined!" Janet cried.

"It's not your fault, Janet," Lisa told her.

"The most important thing is that you're safe," Nikki declared.

Katie added, smiling, "And that you always remember the number-one camp rule—"

All the campers chimed in, "Never go anywhere without telling someone!"

Lisa apologized and promised to remember. Then she changed into dry pajamas and crawled under her covers.

Chapter Six

Lisa awoke early. She wanted to be packed
and ready when Barbie called her parents. Rays
of sunlight were just beginning to peek through
the trees. Lisa was so glad the storm was over.
The ride home would be faster in good weather.

While the other girls slept, Lisa quietly
packed her bag. She left a big note for Nikki
and headed for Barbie's office.

"Lisa!" Barbie cried, surprised to see her
so early. "Good morning!"

"I'm all ready," Lisa announced.

"So you've decided to leave? Well, it's still

early," Barbie replied. "Let's give your parents a chance to wake up before I call. In the meantime, maybe you can help me."

Lisa put her bags down. "Okay," she agreed. "I guess I have time."

"I need to bring some things to the Art Barn. We'll be working on a mural today," Barbie said.

"A mural?" Lisa asked.

Barbie told Lisa about her idea of having everyone at camp work together on a wall-size painting. "Since you girls have art first, you'll be in on the planning stages."

"Oh," Lisa replied slowly. "That should be fun. For them, I mean."

"I think so," Barbie said cheerfully. "We'll start sketching it out this morning."

"Well, maybe I could help until it's time to call my mom or my dad," Lisa offered.

Lisa and Barbie carried the paints down the path toward the Art Barn. All of a sudden, Lisa heard a small noise from above. *Cheep! Cheep!*

"Wait a minute, Barbie," Lisa said, stopping. She looked up and noticed a bird peeking out of its nest. "That's her!" she cried.

"That's who?" asked Barbie.

"The mother bird," Lisa replied. She told Barbie about her discovery of the two birds. She explained how upset she had been that the mother bird might have pushed her baby out of its nest. She said how worried about it she'd been during the storm.

Barbie listened closely. Then she smiled and said, "Now you know how we felt when you were lost. Think about it. You are like that little bird. Your parents pushed you out of the nest to give you a chance to fly. They weren't sending you *away* from home. They were sending you *to* camp.

They hoped you'd have fun here. I had hoped you would, too."

Just then a flutter of wings caught their attention. It was the little bird, flying back home to its mother!

"You did it!" Lisa told the bird. "You're flying!"

Barbie put her arm around Lisa and added, "And so can you, if you try."

Then a voice from down the path called, "There you are!" It was Nikki. "I saw your note. I wanted to make sure we hadn't lost you again!"

"Lisa just wanted to get an early start today," Barbie explained. "She's helping me get the supplies for the mural."

"I haven't told the girls yet," Nikki said.

"What girls?" Katie broke in. She, Janet, and Amanda were hurrying down the path, too.

Amanda scolded Nikki and Lisa. "We woke up, and you guys were gone! After last night, we didn't know what was going on."

"Well, what *is* going on?" Janet asked.

"It's not what's going *on*," Barbie explained. "It's what's going *up!* We're going to make a mural together for the farewell campfire."

"Oh, what fun!" Amanda exclaimed.

"I'll help!" Janet declared.

"We'll all help, won't we, Lisa?" Katie asked. "You're the best artist here."

"Well, maybe for a while," Lisa agreed **hesitantly.** "I'm going home today."

"Oh," Katie said. "You are?"

"But we were going to ask Barbie to take us into town today to buy you a new sketchbook!" Janet blurted out.

Lisa looked surprised. "Wow! You would do that for me?" she asked.

"Sure, you're one of us," Amanda replied.

"We'd better get going," Nikki suggested. "Or else the Tardy Turtles are going to beat us to the Art Barn."

51

Everyone helped carry the supplies. They made it inside just as the Tardy Turtles were stepping in the door. Barbie quickly filled the boys in on the mural project. Without wasting a minute, all the campers began working together.

"I'll do a scene of me swimming faster than you, Brad," Katie joked.

"And I'll do a scene with me putting a skunk in your cabin," Brad shot back.

As they worked, talked, and laughed, the campers forgot about the rainy days and the gloomy moods. It wasn't until the cleanup bell rang that they even thought about stopping work on the mural. Nobody wanted to quit.

Barbie asked the cabin counselors to stay with the campers. Then she slipped out of the studio and hurried toward the Food Barn.

Lisa saw Barbie leave and followed her. "Wait!" she called.

Barbie stopped and turned around.

"You're not going to call my parents, are you?" Lisa asked.

"I was just going to get some more paints," Barbie explained. "But thanks for reminding me."

Lisa was quiet for a moment. The night before, she had had every reason to leave. But now she was starting to realize that she had more reasons to stay. "Maybe you shouldn't call my parents yet."

"But I thought you wanted to go home," Barbie said.

Lisa thought hard. "I've realized that home is any place your heart is," she said. Then she grinned. "And it's okay that my heart is a little bit everywhere. At Mom's, Dad's, and even here at Camp Sunnydale."

Barbie smiled warmly at Lisa. "I'm glad."

"Me, too," Lisa said. And this time she really did mean it.